Art Works™ Drawing Robots

Carolyn Scrace

A⁺

Smart Apple Media

Author:
Carolyn Scrace graduated from Brighton College of Art, England, after studying design and illustration. She has since worked in animation, advertising, and children's publishing. She has a special interest in natural history and has written many books on the subject, including *Lion Journal*, and *Gorilla Journal* in the *Animal Journal* series.

How to use this book:

Follow the easy, numbered instructions. Simple step-by-step stages enable budding young artists to create their own amazing drawings.

What you will need:

1. Paper.
2. Wax crayons.
3. Felt-tip pens to add color.

Published by Smart Apple Media,
an imprint of Black Rabbit Books
P.O. Box 3263, Mankato, Minnesota 56002
www.blackrabbitbooks.com

Published by arrangement with
The Salariya Book Company Ltd

Cataloging-in-Publication Data is available from the Library of Congress

Printed in the United States
At Corporate Graphics,
North Mankato, Minnesota

9 8 7 6 5 4 3 2 1

ISBN: 978-1-62588-347-6

Contents

Clunk!

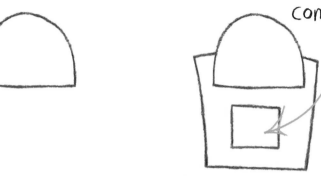

control panel

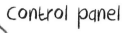

1 Clunk needs a head,

2 ...a body and a control panel,

3 ...two legs and feet,

4 ...one small arm and hand,

5 ...and one **big** arm and hand!

6 Draw in his eyes, nose, and mouth.

Draw in
his two
antennae.

Add crayoned stripes
to Clunk's arms.

Finish drawing
his eyes and
mouth.

Add some dials
and stripes to his
control panel.

Color in with
felt-tip pens.

5

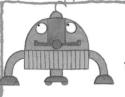

Click!

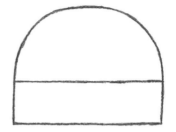

1 Click needs a **big** head,

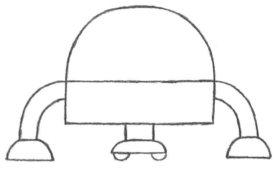

2 ...a body,

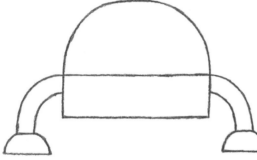

3 ...two arms and hands,

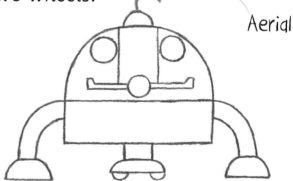

4 ...and a leg with two wheels.

Aerial

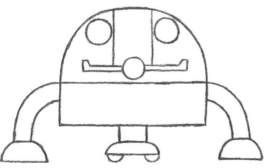

5 Add two eyes and a mouth,

6 ...and draw in her squiggly aerial.

6

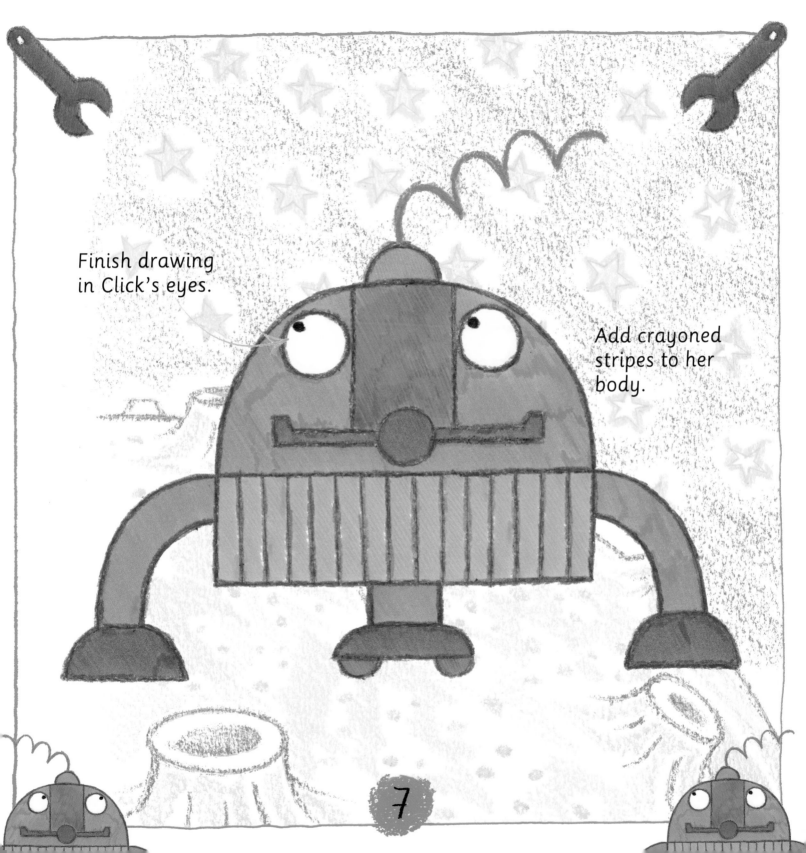

Finish drawing in Click's eyes.

Add crayoned stripes to her body.

7

Buzz!

control panels

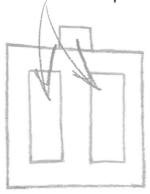

1 Buzz needs a very, very small head,

2 ...a **big** body with two control panels,

3 ...two short legs and feet,

4 ...a long arm and hand and a little one!

5 Now draw in his eyes, ears, and mouth.

6 Add a row of buttons to each control panel.

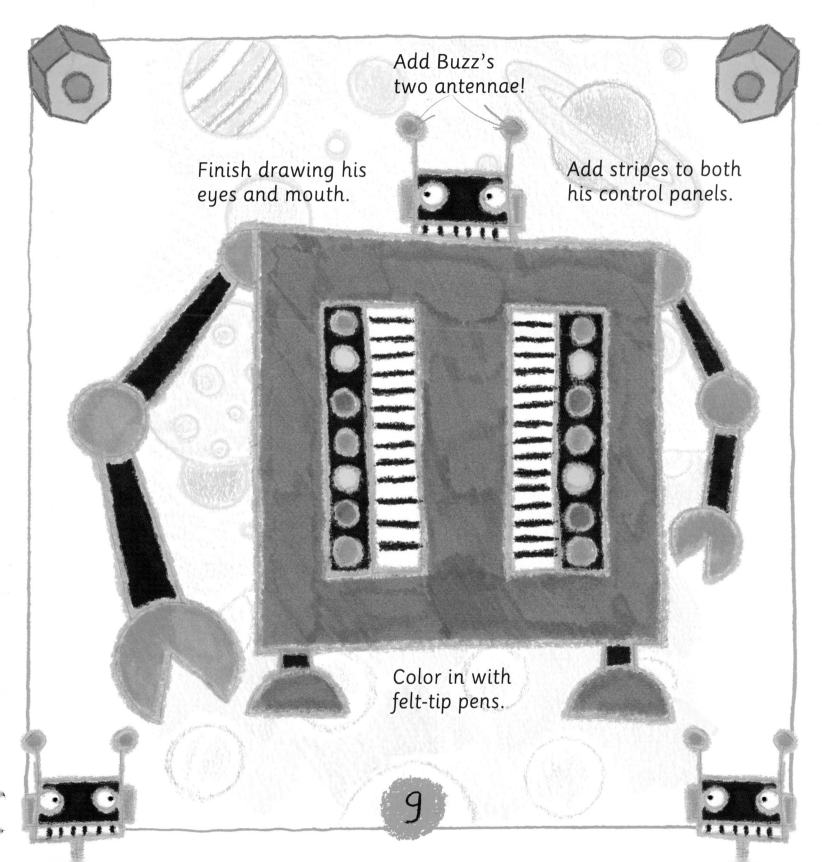

Add Buzz's
two antennae!

Finish drawing his
eyes and mouth.

Add stripes to both
his control panels.

Color in with
felt-tip pens.

Ping!

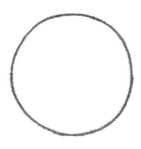

1 Ping needs a body,

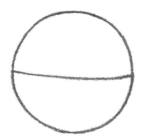

2 ...a head,

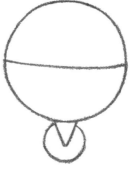

3 ...a little wheel,

4 ...and two big arms and hands.

5 Draw in Ping's face, eyes, and nose,

6 ...and his mouth and two ears!

10

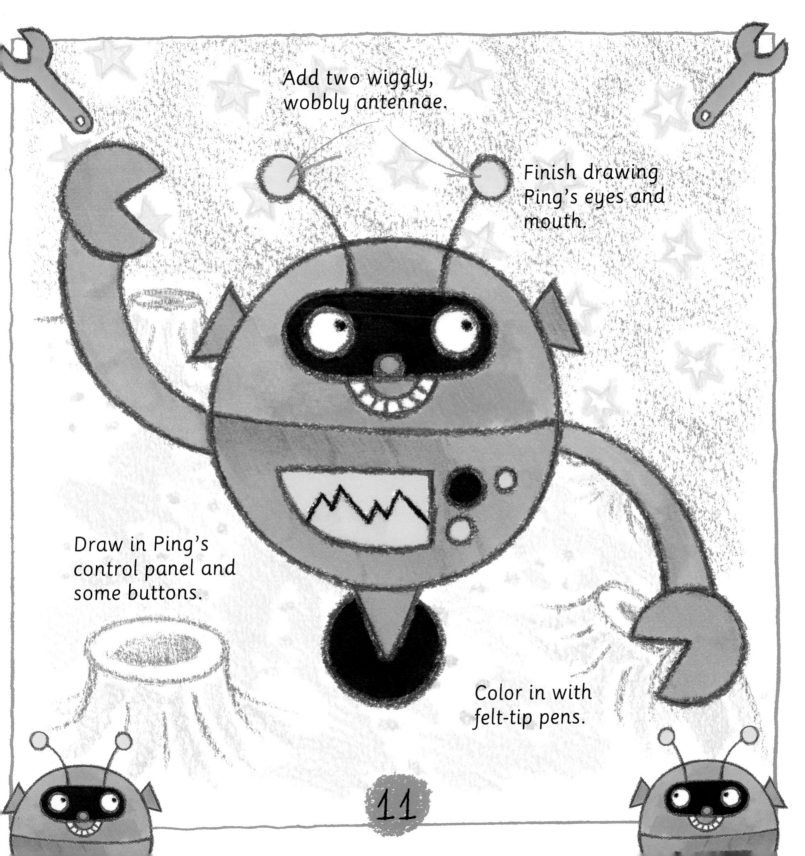

Hiss!

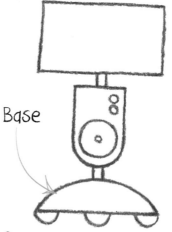

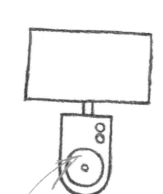

Dial

Base

1 Hiss needs a head, a neck,

2 ...and a body with a dial and two buttons.

3 Now add a base with three wheels,

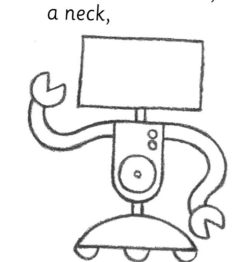

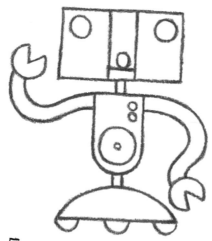

4 ...and two bendy arms and hands.

5 Draw Hiss's eyes, nose, and mouth,

6 ...and add two ears and her antennae!

12

Brackets

Add two brackets on top of her head joined by a curly wire!

Finish drawing Hiss's eyes.

Use a crayon to draw in stripes on her arms.

Add hands to the round dial.

Color in with felt-tip pens.

13

Whiz!

1 Whiz needs a head and neck,

2 ...a body and a control panel,

3 ...**three** legs and feet,

4 ...and two arms and hands.

5 Now draw in two eyes and a mouth,

6 ...and antennae on each side of his head!

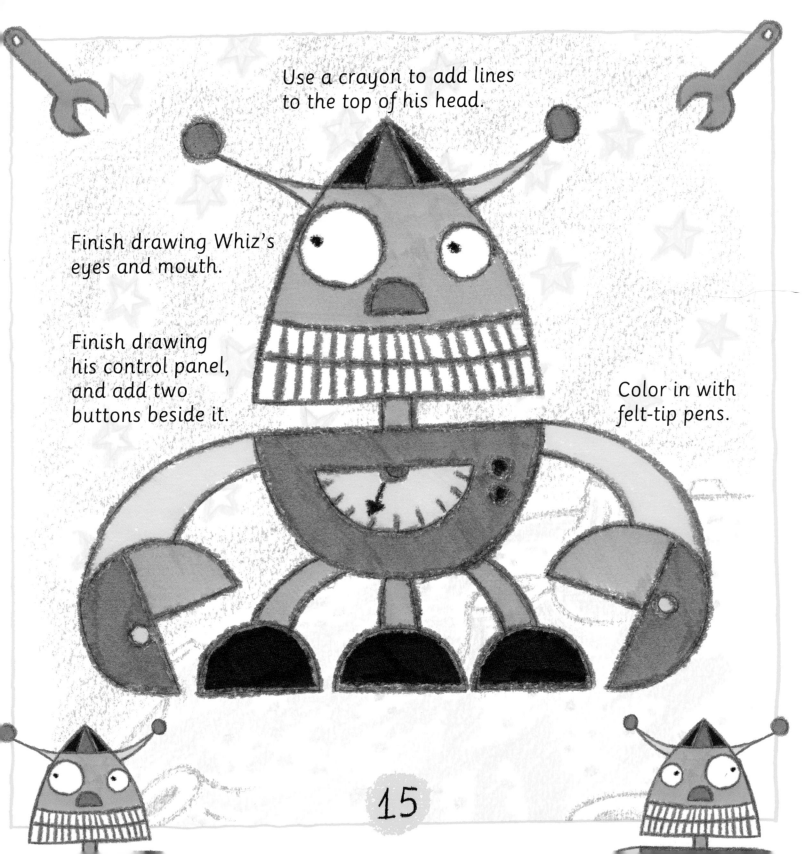

Use a crayon to add lines to the top of his head.

Finish drawing Whiz's eyes and mouth.

Finish drawing his control panel, and add two buttons beside it.

Color in with felt-tip pens.

Purp!

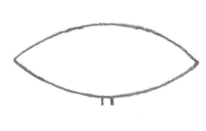

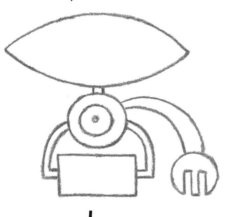 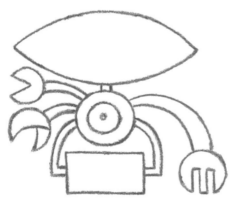 

1 Purp needs a **big** head with a small neck,

2 ...a body with a dial,

3 ...clamps and a roller,

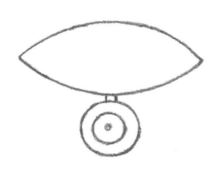 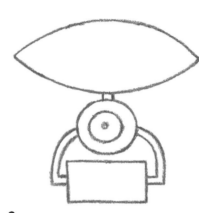

4 ...one **long** arm and a big hand,

5 ...and two small arms and hands.

6 Now draw in her eyes, nose, and very wide mouth!

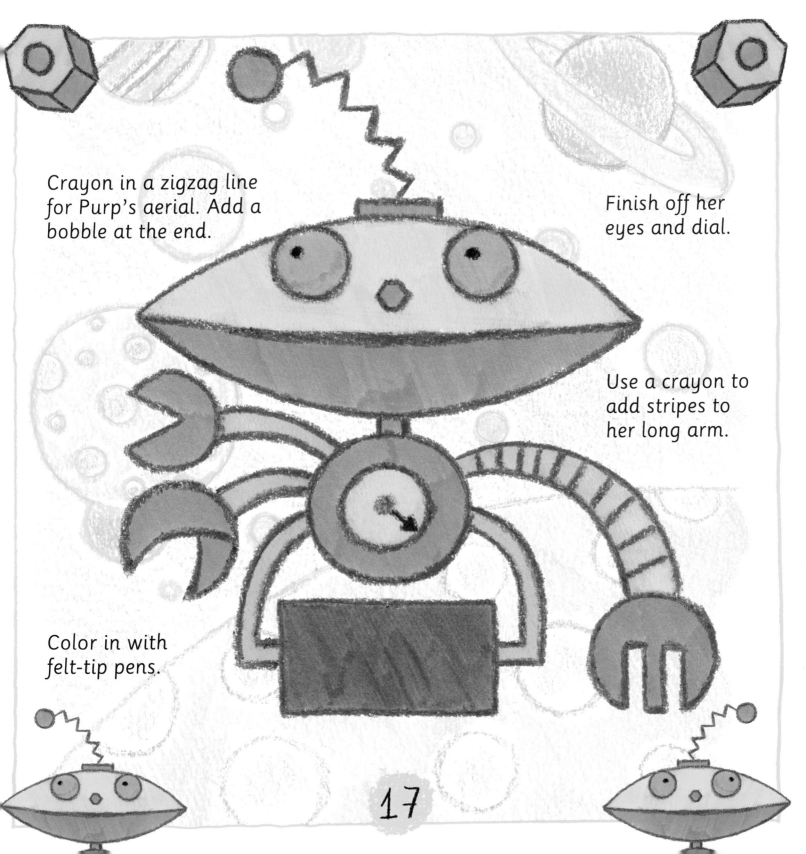

Crayon in a zigzag line for Purp's aerial. Add a bobble at the end.

Finish off her eyes and dial.

Use a crayon to add stripes to her long arm.

Color in with felt-tip pens.

17

 # Bleep!

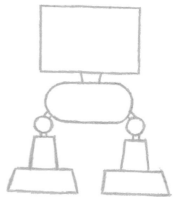

1 Bleep needs a head and neck,

2 ...a body,

3 ...two legs and feet,

Eye sockets

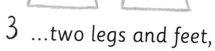

Antennae

4 ...and three arms and hands.

5 Add his eye sockets, eyes, a nose, and mouth,

6 ...and two ears and antennae.

18

Finish drawing
Bleep's eyes.

Use a crayon
to draw a row
of buttons
on Bleep's
mouth.

Draw in his control
panels and add
stripes.

Color in with
felt-tip pens.

Ting!

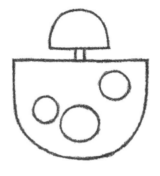

1 Ting needs a head and neck,

2 ...a **big** body with three dials,

3 ...one fat wheel,

Axle   Axle

4 ...with two axles.

5 Add a big arm and hand and a small one,

6 ...and draw one big eye and her mouth.

Antenna

Use a crayon to add one antenna to either side of Ting's head, and another one on top.

Add a third antenna on top of her head.

Finish drawing her eye and the three dials.

Color in with felt-tip pens.

Zap!

control panel

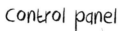

1 Zap needs a head,

2 ...a body and a control panel,

3 ...legs, **knobbly** knees and feet,

Antennae

4 ...and two arms and hands.

5 Draw in her eyes, nose, and mouth,

6 ...and two antennae.

Finish drawing Zap's eyes.

Use a crayon to add dials and switches to her control panel.

Color in with felt-tip pens.

23

Clack!

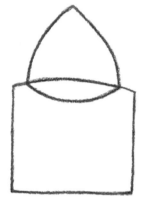

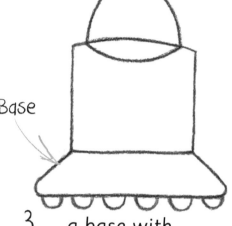

Base

1 Clack needs a head,

2 ...a square body,

3 ...a base with **six** wheels,

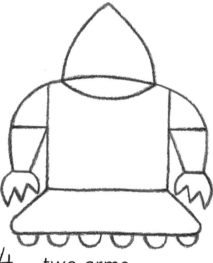

control panel

4 ...two arms and hands,

5 ...and two eyes and ears!

6 Draw in his control panel and buttons.

24

Finish drawing Clack's eyes and teeth.

Add stripes to his control panel using a crayon.

Color in with felt-tip pens.

 # Tick!

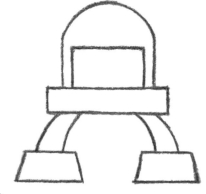

1 Tick needs a head, a box-shaped face,

2 ...a little body,

3 ...two legs with big feet,

Helmet   Antennae

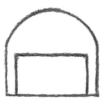

4 ...and two small arms and hands.

5 Draw in his eyes, nose, and mouth,

6 ...a helmet and two antennae!

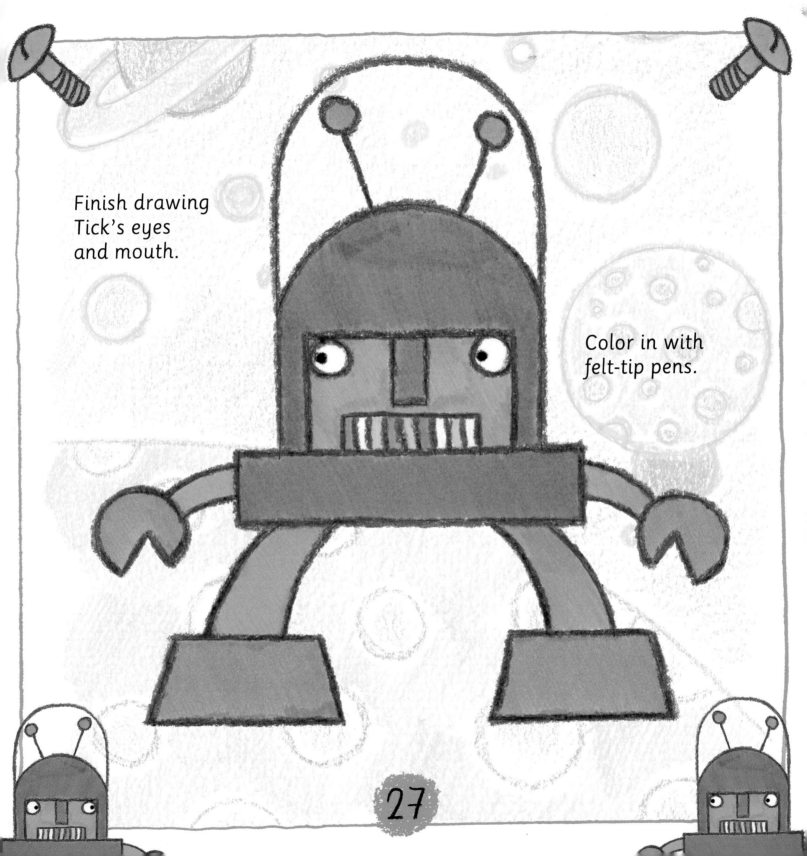

Finish drawing
Tick's eyes
and mouth.

Color in with
felt-tip pens.

Tock!

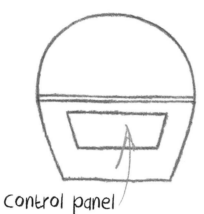

Caterpillar track

Control panel

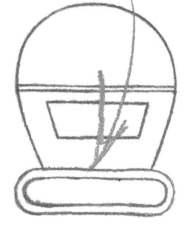

1 Tock needs a head,

2 ...a body and a control panel,

3 ...and a **caterpillar** track,

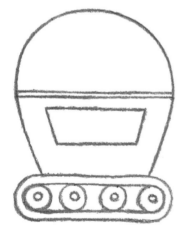

4 ...with four wheels.

5 Now draw in his two arms and hands,

6 ...two eyes, a nose, and a mouth.

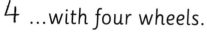

Use crayon to add Tock's two aerials with a zigzag line between them.

Aerials

Finish drawing his eyes.

Add stripes to his control panel.

Add three buttons.

Color in with felt-tip pens.

29

 # Snap!

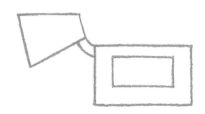

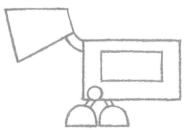

1 Snap needs a head and a neck,

2 ...a body and a control panel,

3 ...two front legs with **big** paws,

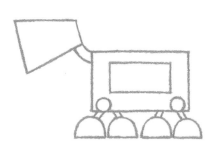

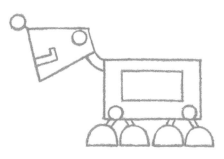

4 ...and two back legs and paws!

5 Draw in his eye, nose, and mouth,

6 ...and his two ears and zigzag tail.

Draw in Snap's teeth
and add his eye.

To finish his control
panel, use a crayon to
add stripes, a dial, and
some buttons.

Color in with
felt-tip pens.

31

Glossary

Antennae feelers.

Axle the rod that a robot's wheels are mounted on.

Caterpillar track a loop of metal or rubber plates that helps a robot to travel on rough ground.

Control panel the part of a robot (or other machine) that has switches or buttons to tell the robot what to do.

Dial a device like a clock face that gives information about speed, pressure, etc.

Eye sockets the parts of a robot's or animal's head that the eyes fit into.

Helmet a hard hat to protect the head.

Roller a very wide wheel for use on smooth ground.

Index